Leah Gwaltney and Eric are best friends and have been since freshman year. Eric wants more than friendship but is willing to wait. Leah wants to love Eric. He is her best friend and she cares about him, but something is missing. There is no electricity between them.

Leah discovers what she has been missing when she meets David Leitner, the handsome graduate student who is old enough to be her father. Instantly and powerfully attracted to each other, they play a titillating game of cat and mouse while he does his best to do the right thing.

Eventually, Leah is forced to take things into her own hands and show him that not only does she know what she wants, but she knows how to get it. In a happy-for-now ending, they discover love does not have an age limit.

Hot For Teacher
Copyright © 2019 Kandeis Lynne
ISBN: 978-1-4874-2387-2
Cover art by Angela Waters

Published by eXtasy Books Inc or
Devine Destinies, an imprint of eXtasy Books Inc

Look for us online at:
www.eXtasybooks.com or www.devinedestinies.com

Hot For Teacher Reading, Writing, and Erotica Book 1

By

Kandeis Lynne

DEDICATION

To my husband, David, and my son, Joshua, thank you for putting up with the late nights and craziness. To my pals, Bill and Peter, thanks for the inspiration.

CHAPTER ONE: ERIC

L eah Gwaltney grinned to herself as she bounced down the stairs of the registration building. The sky was the bright blue that was unique to a Midwestern fall day. The days were still warm, but the breeze reminded her that by evening she would need a sweater. At the bottom of the steps, Leah stepped up onto the stone newel to peer over the crowd of students.

Standing on her tiptoes, Leah craned her head searching for her friend. She was startled when a pair of bold eyes locked onto hers. For a moment, the crowd noise faded and she was captivated. Mr. Green Eyes raised his eyebrows with a mischievous grin that made her feel uncomfortably warm. Embarrassed, Leah looked away. When she dared to glance back up, the handsome stranger was gone.

"What classes did you get?" Eric shouted across the quadrangle. Leah looked around to see her best friend loping across the bricks. His shaggy brown hair flopped in his eyes as he fell into step next to her.

I got Advertising with Weinstein, Set Design, History of Television with Ronald, and Lighting Design with Dr. Sullivan," he continued without allowing her to answer.

"Did you sign up for Ballroom Dancing like I said?" Leah asked.

"Yes, but I don't know why you are making me do this."

"Because you are my friend." Leah smirked.

"Hmph, some friend you are," he grumbled, but Leah could tell he was not really upset. She knew that Eric felt more than friendship for her. She was not sure what she felt for him. She had intentionally avoided examining how she felt too closely. What she knew for sure was that he was her best friend and that he would do anything for her.

Eric was six-two to her five-three. His straight brown hair fell over black-rimmed glasses. His big, soft, brown eyes were alight with humor and happiness. In the two years she had known Eric, she had never seen him without a goofy smile and joke. He was an eternal optimist. Leah Gwaltney bounced along beside him, taking two steps to his one. Her long waist-length, dark auburn hair sparkled with copper highlights in the sunlight. Eric's joie de vivre always rubbed off on her, and she smiled happily up at him.

Of course, they were both young, juniors in college, on their own and having the time of their lives. They had no responsibilities except to keep their grades up. The college, or more accurately their parents' tuition payments, fed and housed them. Despite being underage, there was plenty of alcohol around. Pot was easy enough to come by as well. There was always a party somewhere. They had nothing to do but go to classes and enjoy themselves. Why wouldn't they be optimistic?

"So, what did you get?"

"Almost the same schedule, I didn't get the history class though. It was already full. I got Audio Production, and of course . . . Ballroom Dancing."

"That's cool. At least we have most of the same classes."

Leah's eyes sparkled as she grinned up at him. "Hey, do you know what day it is?"

"Wednesday?"

"And what do we do on Wednesdays?" She laughed.

Together they shouted, "BMW—*Bloody Mary Wednesdays!*"

The Bloody Mary Wednesday tradition had started early

in their freshman year. In an attempt to avoid the lab science requirement, they had both signed up for a computer programming class. The class had been a disaster. The professor had been a dumpy little man with a bad blond comb-over and a closet full of plaid shirts. He clearly did not prepare for his class, or maybe he was just scatterbrained. His lessons were confusing and even, occasionally, wrong. He would write something on the chalkboard and just as students were scurrying to copy it down, he would mumble, "No, no, that's not right," and erase it.

The class was a *weeding out* course, meant to discourage students who were not committed to studying computer science. Eric and Leah were the exceptions in the room. Neither had any intention of pursuing computer science. Taking computer *science* was just a convenient loophole to avoid the onerous Biology or Chemistry 101 that every other freshman was required to take.

The class was held in a huge musty auditorium on the bottom floor of the sciences building. With over three hundred students in the class, asking questions was impossible. Leah had no tolerance for poor teaching. Valedictorian at her high school, Leah had always pushed herself academically. She spent her summers studying Latin, which was not offered at her high school, and reading voraciously. She suffered through the first two classes of Fortran hoping the professor would find his groove. During the third class, she noticed the cute but nerdy young man who had sat next to her in the front row every week.

Noticing her looking at him, he whispered, "This guy really sucks, doesn't he?"

"No kidding. The TAs do a better job than he does." TAs, or teaching assistants, were graduate students that supervised and taught the lab portion of the class. Freshmen quickly learned that the TAs were often better teachers than

3

the professor, and far more accessible.

"You want to ditch?"

"You mean leave? In the middle of class? Won't we get in trouble?"

"Nah, this is college. Nobody cares if you go to class, as long as you pass the tests."

"Really?"

"Really."

Before she could decide what to do, he reached down to grab her backpack and rose to leave. The professor droned on, oblivious to their departure as the two scurried up the aisle and out into the bright fall sunshine.

"Oh my God." She giggled as they escaped the dark auditorium. "I've never ditched a class in my life."

"They say college is a time to explore new things," he said, smiling at her.

"Okay, now for another new experience. Have you tried Mother's Pizza yet?"

"Uhm, no. But, I've heard it's amazing."

Mother's Pizza was a college institution. Stone-baked margherita pizza with fresh house-made mozzarella and basil from the garden behind the shop—Mother's Pizza was legendary.

"Well, come on then. I'm going to bust your pizza cherry."

Leah blushed and looked down at the off-color remark. When she glanced up though, she realized her new young friend was just as mortified as she was.

"Yeah, sorry about that. It sounded better in my head."

At that admission, their friendship was forged. They became inseparable. Mother's Pizza became a Wednesday tradition. They would attend class until the professor's nonsense was unbearable and then depart for Mother's. Eric had a fake ID, and so Bloody Marys became the drink of the day.

Eric actually preferred gin and later tried to establish a *Gin and Tonic Tuesday*, but it never stuck. Every Wednesday that semester, they ate slices and drank Bloody Marys. Sometimes they made it to their next classes, but sometimes they didn't. BMW became a tradition that cemented their friendship and determined their class schedules for years to come.

CHAPTER TWO: FIRST CLASS

Leah smiled as she pushed her way through the heavy, soundproof door to Studio Five. Freshman year, Studio Five had seemed like a magical and mysterious place, but by their junior year, Eric and Leah had spent endless hours in the facility, and it was like a second home to them. Leah's eyes slid around the room, caressing each familiar item. How many times had she raised and lowered the battens to hang lights or moved the massive velvet curtain that surrounded the interior of the studio? Just that weekend, she had sat in the control room and run the Chroma Key, or green screen, for a student project.

Striding across the empty studio, Leah rapped on the large glass window of the lighting control room. Dr. Sullivan, or Sully as he preferred, waved back at her. Between the two control rooms was a small temporary office walled in with cheap plastic panels. The office had been an afterthought when office space for graduate students had run short. Massive twenty-foot rolling ladders hid in dark corners along with rolling storage bins of lighting gels, scrims, filters, and tools.

Leah loved this familiar space, especially when she was alone. The velvet curtains enveloped the room in a climate-controlled peacefulness that was seldom available on a busy college campus. In addition to the countless projects she and Eric had worked on in this studio, they were both members of the production club. Even their weekends and nights were often spent in this space.

Leah arrived early, as usual, and found a spot atop one of the lighting ladders to perch and wait. From here she could see everyone as they entered the studio but, unless someone looked up, she was invisible. Consequently, she was surprised when a voice interrupted her solitude.

"Hey, you mind giving me a hand?" a voice asked from the hall doorway behind the curtain.

As she climbed down and rounded the studio curtain, she said, "Sure, but how did . . ."

The handsome stranger she had noticed in the quad smiled and said, "That's one of my favorite places, too. It's kind of a private space in the middle of everything."

Leah agreed as they manhandled a rolling cart with a big-screen television across the threshold and into the center of the studio.

"Hi, I'm David. My friends call me Dave." As he stuck his hand out to shake hers, Leah faltered. A frisson of pleasure jolted through her when their hands touched. As she looked up into his lazy green eyes, she could tell that he had felt it, too.

"Uhm, I am Leah. My friends call me . . . well . . . Leah."

"So Well-Leah, I'm new here. Are you a graduate student?" he asked.

Before she could answer, she was startled as she felt someone's hand slide down her back. Almost immediately she knew it was Eric. No one else would touch her with such casual intimacy. Leah watched with curiosity as the two men sized each other up. It seemed that an entire conversation had taken place between them in a single moment.

Leah felt David's gaze follow them as they claimed folding chairs in the front row. Leah, unsettled by the awkward moment, was only half listening to Eric as they waited for class to begin.

"So, you'll go to the dance with me? As a friend, I mean?"

Eric asked.

"Sure, sounds like fun." But their easy friendship seemed a little dull after the electric shock of David's touch.

"Okay, gang," David announced from the front of the class. "As you can guess, I am not Professor Wang." A groan went up from the group. "Dr. Wang was offered a fellowship at Ohio State and they did not have time to change the class listing. So . . . you are stuck with little ol' me."

"My name is David Leitner. I am a graduate student in television production. I worked for an advertising agency in New Jersey for three years, then at a public television station in Boston for five more before I decided to go back to school and get my doctorate." David named a very prestigious Boston station. Leah was impressed.

Students around them shuffled and mumbled, unsure what this change meant. Leah's heart pounded. She would see him again—several times a week for the next semester, in fact! She couldn't help but look forward to admiring him from afar. She found him very, very attractive. This class just got a lot more interesting.

Leah did her best to keep her eyes on the television or on her notes as David ran through several recorded advertisements and explained how they had been developed. The one time she dared to glance up, she caught his eye and he winked at her. It was a subtle wink, but definitely a wink. She felt her face flush and a warmth between her legs that made her squirm uncomfortably in the cold metal chair. She had never been affected by a man like this. He was old enough to be her father. He even had a few gray hairs sprinkled in his dark wavy hair. The grin on his face made it clear to her that he knew exactly how he was affecting her.

Eric's voice brought her crashing back to Earth from her fantasy with the very sexy David Leitner.

"You want to get a slice after class?"

"No, not tonight. I, uhm, I'm not feeling great," she lied.

"Yeah, you do look a little flushed," Eric sympathized. "Your face is all pink."

Shrugging him off, Leah said, "I'll be fine. I think I just need some sleep."

"Yeah, okay. Hey, I'll call you tomorrow with the details about the dance."

"Whah?" Leah started but recalling their earlier conversation, she smiled and said, "Great, thanks."

Eric waved and shouted a sympathetic, "Hope you get to feeling better soon." Leah noted with dismay that Eric's touch had elicited nothing more than mild annoyance at his mothering.

CHAPTER THREE: THE CHOICE

The next few days, Leah found herself constantly distract-ed by the attractive production instructor. Between clas-ses, she made excuses to be in Studio Five but did not man-age to run into him. When the next class met, she was disap-pointed, then annoyed, to find that a guest speaker was cov-ering the class.

"I wonder where Mr. Leitner was tonight," Eric said through a mouthful of pizza after class.

"How would I know?" Leah asked irritably.

"Geez, who peed in your Cheerios?"

Seeing the hurt look on his face, Leah relented. After all, she could fantasize about the delicious David Leitner, but nothing was ever going to happen. Right? Here was sweet, kind, thoughtful Eric who would do anything for her and she was being hateful to him.

"Sorry," Leah offered, reaching over to touch his hand.

Eric immediately brightened and asked, "Have you de-cided what you are wearing to the dance?"

"Pink, I think. It's a hot pink, not a baby pink. What about you? Are you wearing a suit or a tux?" she asked as she poured herself another drink from the pitcher they were splitting.

"I thought I'd rent a black tux with tails, and I've got a li-mo lined up to take us to the dance!"

"Are you going to wear a bow tie?" Leah asked with a wink. Eric would be adorable in a bow tie. His tall, thin, gangly frame, shaggy hair, and glasses gave him a hipster vibe, but his deep brown eyes and heart-on-his-sleeve personality made her think of a big, sloppy, sweet sheepdog. She knew that Eric wanted more from her, but he had never pushed.

She wanted to love him. She did love him, in a way. He was sweet, smart, funny, and her best friend. He had even kissed her once. It had been nice. Being with Eric would be like that kiss — nice. But, they were friends, and as long as neither of them acknowledged this other feeling, they could just stay friends.

"I'll pick you up at five on Friday. Okay?"

"Why so early? I thought the dance wasn't until seven."

"Pictures. They want all of the Beta Rho Beta brothers to meet in the field below the library for pictures with their dates."

"Ugh! The things I do for a friend!" Leah said in mock exasperation.

Eric laughed, but she knew she had stung him a little with the friend comment.

"Hey, let's go smoke a little," Leah said, changing the subject abruptly. "Have you got any?"

"Yeah, I've got some in my room at the house. Come on. You can stay over."

Still feeling annoyed at David's absence and repentant for mistreating Eric, Leah recklessly followed him to the fraternity house. In the back of her head, she knew this was not the right move, but she was a little bit drunk from the Sangria and a whole lot horny.

Eric ran his roommate out for the night and placed a tie on the doorknob — the universal college symbol for *Do Not Disturb*. This was not the first time Leah had spent the night at the Beta Rho Beta house. Several times, they had snuggled after a night of drinking or crashed after working late on a project. It had never gone further than a kiss. Spooning with

Eric, she had been well aware that he wanted more, but she had feigned sleep or drunkenness to put him off. Other men might have considered her a tease. She really didn't mean to lead him on. She just wasn't sure what she wanted, and Eric was willing to wait.

Tonight was different. Leah had spent almost a week in a state of perpetual arousal. Eric was not David. But, she thought dismally, David was out of her league. He was a graduate student. He was much older than she was. He was her instructor. For so many reasons, David was never going to happen. And more importantly at the moment, Eric was here, and David was not. As Eric packed a bowl in his homemade bong, Leah told herself to forget David Leitner and focus on her very willing friend, Eric.

Pot made Leah tumescent. Considering that she had spent the week wound tight as a drum, it didn't take much for her to make a move on Eric. Between bowls, she slid into his arms as he lay back on his bed contentedly stoned. Surreptitiously, she began running her fingers across his chest. Slowly she worked her way down to his waistband and slid her fingers back and forth along the exposed skin at the top of his jeans. His body responded faster than his brain did. Moving her head to his chest, she could see his cock jerking to attention as she moved her strokes beneath his waistband.

By the time Eric tensed and looked at her with the question in his eyes, Leah was too far gone to stop. Sliding down his body, she unzipped his fly and tugged on his jeans. He lifted his ass to allow his jeans and boxers to slide down. She breathed in the warm sexual smell of him and wrapped her hands around his now fully alert cock. Slowly, she lowered her mouth onto him and allowed his dick to fill her to the back of her throat.

She heard Eric gasp and she grinned a little. She was good at this. She knew what guys wanted. She knew most girls didn't like to do this, but she did. She liked the powerful feeling it gave her. Using her lips and teeth, she slid her mouth up and down his rockhard shaft. She could feel him writhing below her. She also knew that he had not been with anyone like this in a long time. If she didn't take it easy on him, it would be over too soon, and she had not gotten what she needed yet. Leah felt him arching into her and knew he was close to losing control. Grabbing her head between his hands, Eric panted, "Stop, you're going to kill me!"

Pulling her up to his face, he kissed her, tenderly at first, then with growing passion. Briefly her mind flitted to David, but she forced herself to stay in the moment. Clumsily, he worked loose the buttons on her blouse and unhooked her bra, tossing both on the floor. Grasping her breasts with his hands, he murmured, "Beautiful." She assumed he was referring to her anatomy, but when she looked up he was staring directly into her eyes and said again, "You are so beautiful."

Embarrassed, she turned her head and started to work her way down to his impatient cock, but he stopped her. "Oh no you don't! It is my turn."

Eric jumped off the bed and approached her from the foot of the bed. Sliding her knees up and her legs apart, she watched him ease one finger, then two inside her. She knew she was soft, wet, and ready.

"Oh God, you feel good," he groaned.

Watching his fingers move in and out of her, Leah gasped when he began to move his thumb over her clitoris. Her tiny nub was hard and erect. Above him, Leah pulled her nipples until they were hard as pebbles. Leah saw him gasp when he noticed her pleasuring herself.

Finding a rhythm, he stroked and plunged until she began to whimper. "Now! Fuck me now!" she cried out.

He crawled back up to her and kissed her once before she

reached for his cock. Raising her hips to meet him, she took the matter into her own hands. He was unable to resist as her wet, warmth enveloped him. After a few moments of stroke and counter stroke, they found their tempo. He was clearly worshipping her body with his. She saw the love and felt his adoration in each touch. But then the barrier was breached, and they were lost in the pulsing mist of desire.

Spent, she snuggled against him as he pulled the cover over their naked bodies. He stroked her hair and whispered, "I think I love you." Leah closed her eyes and pretended to sleep. She did not know how to answer him. *Do I love Eric? Can I love Eric and still want David?*

Leah felt guilty about how she had used Eric. *Used* was the only word for it. She had relieved her own sexual frustration by seducing Eric. Even worse, Eric now believed there was something between them. The sex had been powerful. But, there had been no electricity. She could have accomplished what he did with her vibrator. She did not desire Eric. She tried not to finish the sentence in her head, *like she desired David*. She had used her friend and that made her a bad person.

As she felt tears well behind her closed eyes, she knew the answers to her questions were not the one Eric was hoping for.

CHAPTER FOUR: THE DANCE

Eric, oblivious to Leah's second thoughts, was elated as he picked her up for the dance. He felt set free to declare the love that he had felt growing since the first time he met her. He had already told her once, but she had been asleep. He would tell her again tonight. He would pick her up in a big black limousine, give her a beautiful corsage, and sweep her off her feet. He knew she had been reticent about becoming more than friends, but he felt like a corner had been turned. He would tell her that he loved her and he would make her as happy as he was. He would make her love him.

Eric escorted a reluctant Leah from the limo to the open field below the library for pictures. Eric knew she despised being photographed, but the photographer was good, and soon had her laughing and smiling for the camera. She and Eric made a handsome couple. He looked dapper in his tuxedo and top hat, and her hot pink metallic dress revealed a generous view of her breasts before it belled out to a full skirt.

Leah was starting to relax and look forward to the evening when she heard Eric call out, "Hey, Mr. Leitner, we missed you last week." She turned to look into David's burning green eyes. He spoke to Eric, but he never looked away from Leah. She could not look away either. It was there between them. Electricity. Desire. Wanting. Need. This time there was no denying it. Without even touching her, he set her on fire.

Finally, with a small grimace he turned to face Eric.

"She looks beautiful!"

"Yes, she does!" Eric replied, putting his arm possessively around her.

Capitulating to Eric apparent claim on her, Leah saw David nudge Eric's shoulder with a false heartiness and tease, "Don't do anything I wouldn't do!"

Responding to the old joke, Eric replied, "If we do, we'll name it after you!"

Fraternity dances, no matter how fancy, all smelled the same—sweat, cheap beer, and urine. The Beta Rho Beta formal was no exception. The Beta Rho Beta sweethearts had decorated the hotel ballroom room with a few fake palm trees, tissue paper flowers, and plastic leis. Plastic pineapples filled with punch—cheap grain alcohol and cherry drink mix—were thrust into their hands as they entered the room.

The band had already started and sounded pretty good. They were running through the regular college dance anthems designed to get everyone dancing, drinking, and later fucking. "Cadillac Ranch" was guaranteed to get everyone on the floor—you didn't have to be able to dance to bounce along and shout the lyrics. Soon they would play "Mony, Mony" by Billy Idol. No one actually knew the real lyrics to this song but *You make me feel . . . fuckin' horny, fuckin' horny, fuckin' horny!* was always shouted over the music.

A banner over the bandstand proudly announced the theme of the formal, *Let's Get Lei-d!* Leah knew Eric expected to do exactly that tonight. She could not surrender to her body tonight. It was not fair to Eric and, though it eased her ache temporarily, it only served to stoke her desire for David, and that was definitely not fair to Eric. In her remorse, she had given a great deal of thought on how to deal with tonight. She knew tonight was headed somewhere she was not prepared to go.

Plan one was to get so drunk that nothing could happen. If she was pounding the drinks, then so would Eric. This was a dangerous plan. She would have to keep them at the dance until they were insensible. If she let him get her alone, the drinks would accomplish the opposite of her plan, lowering her inhibitions and soon after that, her panties.

Plan two was the backup plan of every pretty girl—tears. She would tearfully confess that she *loved him like a friend and that it was her, not him.* A completely lame plan but ironically quite true.

Despite her guilty conscience, after a few cups of punch, Leah was actually having a good time. Eric was her best friend, and they always had a good time together. They danced and laughed. Eric hadn't even tried to kiss her. He held her close when they slow danced but so did the other fraternity boys when she danced with them. One or two of them had tried to kiss her or grab her ass drunkenly, but Eric had been the ultimate gentleman, keeping his hands and his lips to himself.

"Hey," Leah shouted over Mellencamp, "they are doing shots over there. Let's go do one!" For some reason, guys found girls doing shots very sexy. Leah wasn't sure if it was because the alcohol was strong and the guys thought it was tough, or maybe it was the salt licking that the guys found erotic. It was more likely that shots were a shortcut to getting their date drunk and their getting lei-d. Leah should have remembered that but too many pineapples of punch had weakened her judgment, and so she bounced off the dance floor and dragged Eric behind her to the bar.

"Do a shot with me!" Leah shouted over the music. Eric nodded and indicated two to the Beta Rho Beta brother serving as bartender. Simultaneously, they licked the salt from between their thumb and index finger, downed the tequila and bit into the lemon wedge.

"Lick, sip, suck!" Eric grinned as he slammed his shot glass down. Leah should have heeded the warning as his eyes widened, but she did not.

"Another one!"

Leah was feeling drunk and reckless. Somewhere in the back of her head, a little voice reminded her that she couldn't hurt her friend again, but she was having fun and so she told her little voice to go to hell.

After three quick shots of tequila, she was limp as a noodle. Eric led her to the dance floor and supported her as they swayed to "Lady in Red."

"I think I need to lie down," Leah mumbled, "the room is spinning!"

"Are you going to be sick?"

"No, I'm fine!" Leah announced, abruptly pushing away from Eric's embrace. "I just need to rest a minute." Leah wobbled a few steps, then stumbled as she stepped on the hem of her dress.

"Here, let me help you." He caught her around the waist and pulled her close to his side as he maneuvered them both across the dance floor.

As they reached the edge of the dance floor, Leah stopped and announced boozily, "Wait . . . wait . . . I want to take my shoes off." Without waiting she kicked her high heels off and sent them flying across the room. "Oops!" Leah giggled as one shoe skittered a few feet and the other bounced off a nearby wall.

"Come on, let's get you to bed." Eric sighed.

"Am I gonna get lei-d?"

Eric stopped and looked into her eyes. Giving in momentarily, he kissed her but then pulled away and groaned, "Not while you are this drunk."

As they reached their hotel room, Leah stumbled across the threshold and fell onto the bed. Eric, equally intoxicated but ever the gentleman, positioned a trash can near the edge of the bed and sat down next to her.

"You think I'm drunk, don't you?"

"You are drunk.

"No, I'm not! I'm just slightly intoxicated!" Leah said in mock indignation.

"That's the same thing as drunk!"

"Oh . . . well, then I guess I'm drunk! Here," Leah said, patting a spot next to her on the bed, "come snuggle." Eric hesitated a moment, then slid into the spot she had indicated.

Wrapping his arms around Leah so that they spooned together, Eric sighed and asked, "You know I am in love with you, right?"

Feeling tears pricking her eyelids, Leah could do nothing but nod against his chest.

"But, you are not in love with me, are you?"

Leah tried to speak, tried to say the things she had planned to say, but the lump in her throat was too big. Finally, with tears streaming down her face, she turned to look into his sweet brown eyes and said, "No, not the way you want me to be. I'm sorry . . . I wish . . . it's just . . ."

Eric caught a tear on his fingertip and studied it intently for a moment. Then he reached out and pulled her close and stroked her hair, whispering, "I know. I know. I know. Don't cry. It's okay." After the storm passed, they both slept wrapped in each other's arms. Early in the morning, Eric held her hair while she was sick. Wiping her face with a damp cloth, he soothed her back to sleep, offering the only love she would accept from him — friendship.

On the surface, their relationship was unchanged. They

still ditched classes and went for BMW's. They still laughed and studied together. They were still inseparable, but there was a wall that had never been there before. There was a line that could never be crossed again without hurting someone irreparably. While they still spent time together, they were each watching that they didn't step near that line. This constant diligence made work from what had been effortless. They only spoke once of the night of the dance. One evening, out of the blue, Leah asked, "How did you know?"

Eric, knowing without question what she meant, replied, "I saw how you looked at him. I realized that you had never looked at me like that and I just knew." Leah opened her mouth to deny, to explain, to apologize, but nothing came out. There was nothing to say. Hurting Eric was the worst thing she had ever done but trying to deny the truth would only twist the knife.

CHAPTER FIVE: THE PROJECT

Whatever had passed between David and Leah the night of the dance had seemed to evaporate. David treated Leah like any other student in his class. He seemed to look right through her. And it was pissing her off!

She knew there was something powerful between them and she intended to make him face it. Step one was to give back as good as she was getting. She went back to calling him Mr. Leitner. She looked away whenever his glance skimmed over her. She did her best to pretend he didn't exist. She chatted with the other students in class, seemingly oblivious to his presence. She was certainly not oblivious—every nerve fiber in her body stood at attention when he was near. She could feel the electricity when he walked into the room—even with her back turned—but she wasn't giving in. She knew he wanted her and she was going to make him work for it.

"Okay, gang," David announced from the front of the studio, "be sure to sign up for a time before you leave tonight. You will need to show me your storyboards and lighting plans at your individual conferences."

Leah took her time gathering her things but since she sat in the front of the class and David's office was in the back, it was easy for her to manage to be the last to sign up. "Perfect!" she gloated as she scribbled her name on the last line of the sign-up sheet. "We will see how well he can ignore me when we are alone!"

To avoid acknowledging David, who had just racked the

last folding chair and was headed toward his office door, Leah shouted to a friend making her way out of the studio, "Hey, wait up!" Purposely turning away from David, Leah hurried to her waiting classmate. She was certain that she heard David mumble under his breath, "Well played, Miss Leah, well played." She couldn't help but glance back once with a smirk. She saw only his back as he closed his office door.

Her storyboard conference was two days away. They were two of the longest days of her life. When the hour finally arrived, she felt like she might explode. She had spent every moment of the two days preparing for this meeting. She had spent hours on her storyboard and was justifiably proud of her effort. In any other situation she would have anticipated this meeting, looked forward to the approbation. She had always been strong academically and enjoyed the accolades that came with success. But of course, tonight that was not the only goal she had.

David cleared his throat and began, "So . . . let's see your storyboard." Leah noticed that David had strategically placed himself behind his desk and invited her to sit across from him. Point one—David.

She took the offered seat but pulled it closer to his desk, allowing her to rest her elbows on the desktop, giving him a nice view of her breasts as she leaned over the desk to explain the key elements of her presentation. Point two—Leah.

"I get this part, but can you explain how you plan to shoot this section with only two floor cameras?"

Seizing the opportunity, Leah moved around to David's side of the desk. She could feel the heat radiating from his skin as she leaned over him to explain. Later she could not recall anything she said because all she could hear was the blood pounding in her ears. Even the smell of him set her teeth on edge.

David was equally distracted by her. He knew she was toy-ing with him, but unfortunately it was working. Without looking at her, he ran his thumb across the space between her thumb and index finger. Time stopped. Neither of them spoke.

"You know we can't—I can't—" he growled in frustration "—I am old enough to be your father!" Finally turning to look at her, he asked, "What are you? Twelve?"

The tension relieved, Leah burst out laughing. "What are you? A hundred?"

"I'll have you know I am not one hundred—only ninety-eight! Really, how old are you?"

"Twenty," she replied.

"Jesus! Not even twenty-one! I think it would be a felony if I even kissed you!"

"Not if I let you," Leah offered, staring down at him.

"You are tempting, little Miss Leah! But as much as I would like to kiss you—and I would very much like to kiss you—I cannot. First, you are half my age. Second, you are my student. And third"—he blew out a breath—"shit, there must be a third . . ."

Leah was momentarily taken aback by his bluntness. He was turning her down. She felt humiliation began to creep into her cheeks, but then she looked at David. His mouth may have said *no*, but his eyes did not. Calling his bluff, she leaned in slowly, closing the gap between them. Stopping with her lips just millimeters from his, she whispered, "That's a real shame, Mr. Leitner."

Having won the point, she exited the room without a

word. It wasn't until she felt the cool night air on her burning cheeks that she realized that she had left her storyboard and backpack in his office. She would get them later. Going back now would ruin her dramatic exit.

David blew out his breath. "Damn!" He knew without a doubt that he needed to leave her alone. She was way too young for him. And what about the boy? Eric? Last thing he needed was some teenage fraternity Romeo coming to defend his turf! Or worse yet, her father! No, he knew this was a mistake. He promised himself that he had just ended it. He had shut her down, and her last play was just to save face. But in his groin, he knew she had left the door open and that he would eventually go through it.

CHAPTER SIX: SATURDAY NIGHT

David tried to ignore the empty chair as he began class, but something inside him eased when Leah slipped into the room at the last minute and grinned up at him. Despite the fact that he had, ostensibly, turned her down, a bond had been forged between them. Just admitting their mutual desire had connected them in a way that was more than titillating. David did his best to resist the urge to look at her, but just thinking about her made his mouth water and his crotch ache.

"Miss Gwaltney," David interrupted as she started out the door after class. "May I speak to you before you go?"

David smirked as he saw a blush warming her cheeks. Reaching out to pull her aside, he whispered, "Not so brave with other people around, are you?"

Reclaiming her equilibrium, she smiled sweetly, "I'll keep up."

With a subtle lift of his eyebrow, David said, "Don't worry. All I want to know is if you can run the lighting board for me this weekend. I talked to Sully and he said that you were one of his best students. My tech bailed on me at the last minute and I only have the studio for a few hours this Saturday evening."

"What makes you think I don't have plans this Saturday?" Leah asked defensively.

Thrown off his stride, David glanced at Eric who was glaring impatiently at the two of them from the door. "Oh . . . well . . . do you?"

Leah grinned as she said, "Nah, I'm just messing with you. What time?"

While the air still sizzled between them, David and Leah worked well together. They both knew their jobs and did them well. Leah was impressed with his preparation. He had a well thought-out shot list. His talent was prepared and he had recruited some of the top graduate and undergraduate students to crew. The original tech had already designed the lighting scheme Just lighting a scene was a simple process. The first step was establishing a key, the main source of illumination for the scene. Adding fill and back lights provided depth and dimension to the subject.

Lighting a scene well required vision. A good tech could tell a story with just the lighting. Often directors ignored the impact that it had on the story. "Hang some lights and leave me to tell the story" was their attitude. David obviously knew better and listened when Leah offered a few constructive suggestions.

After hours of shooting, David called a wrap, and everyone jumped in to strike the set. In a professional studio, there would have been a set crew, but in the world of college television production everyone was expected to help out. Dirty, tired, and hungry, the crew sprawled in the studio floor munching Mother's pizza and drinking sodas provided by David in lieu of payment. That was the other thing about college television—everybody worked for free.

Gradually, the crew began to drift off, claiming tests to study for and papers to write. Leah began to gather and stuff the remaining pizza boxes and soda cans into the nearest rolling trash can. In a television studio everything was on wheels: ladders, tool boxes, and yes, even trash cans. Studio Five was a generous space, but as it served as both a semiprofessional production space and a full-time classroom for all of the technical classes, there was no room for large, awkward, or otherwise immovable objects. Surveying the room for errant crusts, Leah cinched the bag shut and struggled to lift it from the huge green rolling bin.

"Needs some help?" David asked.

"No, I've got it!" Leah said while trying unsuccessfully to lift the heavy bag clear of the can. Blowing a strand of dark copper hair from her eyes in frustration, she muttered, "Yes, please. Damn thing weighs a ton."

"It galls you a little to let me help doesn't it?"

"No . . . maybe . . . oh, shut up!" she said in mock irritation at the twinkle of humor in his eyes. Good God, he had sexy eyes. Gray-green, they were the color of worn military fatigues. Her breath caught in her throat a little as she noticed the widening of his pupils and the suddenly overwrought silence that fell between them.

"I . . . uhm . . . I better take this out to the dumpster," David said without breaking eye contact.

"Yeah, you know, mice and everything," Leah breathed.

"Yeah, mice . . ." He sighed. "Wait. What?"

Leah broke the tension by bursting out laughing. "Mice! If you don't take out the trash, the studio will be swarming with mice! They come in through the loading dock!"

As David maneuvered the trash bag to the door, Leah called out, "I'm going to pull the gels now that the lights have cooled down."

"Wait a minute and I'll brace the ladder for you," David offered over his shoulder.

Leah ignored his suggestion as she tugged the giant ladder under the Kleigs she had used during the production. Like everything else, it was on wheels. Sullivan had secured hefty wooden ladders to rolling plywood frames. They were massively heavy and practically impossible to tip over. In addition, she had no fear of heights. She had climbed up with forty pound Fresnel light in one hand so many times that she had lost count.

"Hey, I thought I told you to wait for me."

"I'm . . . almost . . . done."

Leah stretched to retrieve the last colored filter from the frame in front of the concentric lens.

"Heads up!" Leah shouted as she dropped the red and blue plastic filters There was no reason to carry them down the ladder. They were trashed. Filters could only be used so many times before they became brittle and warped. These were at the end of their lifespan and so she allowed them to flutter to the ground rather than carrying them down with her. As she began to back down, she noticed the annoyed look on David's face below her.

"There is no reason to be careless!" David scolded.

"It would take a wrecking ball to knock this thing over!"

"It would not take a wrecking ball for you to fall off of it though!"

Leah halted her progress down when she reached the top of David's head. Turning her back to the ladder, she slid down a step at a time while enunciating with annoyance, "I . . . can . . . take . . . care . . . of . . . my . . . self." On the next to last step she found herself face to face, caged in by his arms,.

Slowly David leaned in to whisper in her ear, "I bet you can, Leah." His hot breath tickled her ear and sent chills down her arms. "And I wouldn't mind watching that at all."

A surge of heat pinked her face as she recognized the double entendre. Never one to back down she turned her face to meet his. Now only inches away, she thought the crackles of electricity must be literally visible. She could feel the heat balloon between them. Judging by the tempo of the pulse throbbing on his neck, she knew she had called his bluff. It was a mistake, however, to let her triumph show with the merest twitch of her lips into a smirk.

He pressed her back against the rungs of the ladder and kissed her. He kissed her desperately. Gentle at first, he soon made clear his desire for her. Darting his tongue into her mouth first, then pulling back to nip at her bottom lip, he groaned. "You are playing with fire!"

"So are you!" she whispered into his ear. Stepping off the final step of the ladder, she allowed her body to slide deliciously down his, settling her need against his. She thought she might actually pass out from the pleasure of it. He kissed her until she was dizzy with wanting him. When at last they parted, they were both breathless. She could feel her shirt sticking to her damp skin.

With a shaky breath, David looked into her eyes again. "This still doesn't change things! We can't . . ."

Leah, still speechless, just nodded. David gave the ladder a slight push, sending her rolling a few feet away. As he turned to walk away, he grinned over his shoulder and said, "And Leitner wins the point!"

For a moment Leah remained frozen, but a smile slowly spread across her face. "Oh game on, David, game on!"

Leaving the studio, Leah mused on the frustrating evening ahead. "Perhaps I could go out, find someone to . . . oh no . . ." she vowed. "This was all his doing and I won't settle. He is going to get everything he has coming." In the meantime, as he had pointed out, "I *can* take care of myself."

The following weeks passed in heat-singed blur. The gauntlet had been thrown and neither would relent. While he continued to resist with his words, his body was clearly in the game. Carelessly he would brush against her as they passed in narrow confines of the editing suite, causing her nipples to leap to attention. Surrounded by other students, she could do nothing but bite her lip and try not to squirm. She returned the favor by "accidentally" leaning against him and grinding her ass into him as she stood in front of him in a crowded elevator. His fingers bit into her arms as he held her there and whispered into her ear, "Don't you dare twitch that sweet little ass one more time!" He continued to hold her in place as the elevator went up and down and up again. Finally, when the last passenger unloaded, she could feel the tension in his arms relax as he released her. Without looking back, Leah licked a finger and drew a tick mark in the air as she left him gaping in the empty elevator.

CHAPTER SEVEN: THE COAST

As the semester drew to a close, Leah pondered what to do for the summer term. She had long since outgrown going home for the summer. Thomas Wolfe was right when he said, "You can never go home again." Leah was unsure if it was her or home that had changed, but she guessed it might be a little of both. Nonetheless, she would stay on campus, take a few classes to justify her parents' tuition check and maybe get a summer job. Her friendship with Eric had survived intact. There was a subtle distance between them that had never existed before, but she had concluded that it was only fair. It would be completely unconscionable for her to breach that wall again. Regardless, she was relieved that he was going to be in New Hampshire the whole summer, working as a counselor for a special needs camp.

Her flirtation with the delicious David Leitner continued to arouse and entertain her. The spring term had offered up a delightful surprise — campus league softball. Leah was fit, but not particularly athletic. As a consequence, she had never bothered to participate in the intercollegiate athletics program. Upon learning that David played shortstop for the telecommunications department team, the Editors, she decided it was high time she developed some team spirit.

Games were usually played on Friday or Saturday afternoons. And goodness, the view was good from the cheap seats! A few of the players were undergraduates working toward BA's in Telecommunications, but most were the graduate students who served as associate instructors, like

David, and the professors that lived on campus year-round. Everyone else was the pep squad.

The department was small and so Leah knew almost everyone. As a result, she was completely comfortable following the crew to Mother's for post-games celebrations. The younger players celebrated if the team won, while the older professors celebrated that they hadn't broken or torn anything important. The majority of the team and entourage was over twenty-one, and since they bought the pitchers of beer, none of the waitresses asked questions. Besides this was a college town, if the waitresses refused to serve anyone underage the restaurants would go bankrupt in days.

"So, Leah, what are you doing this summer?" Vic shouted over the restaurant noise. Vic was a handsome young Italian graduate student in the audio production department. He had a delicious accent and a contagious smile. He had been the TA for her audio production course in the fall. He was an incorrigible flirt and was easy to talk to.

"I don't know. I was kind of thinking of finding a summer job, but I think I may have waited too late to look. You know when all the students go home, a lot of the jobs leave, too," she shouted back, taking a sip of the warm beer.

Vic nudged Dave. "Hey, Dave! This young lady is looking for a summer job. Didn't you just tell me you needed a floor manager for the video you're shooting on the coast next week?"

"Huh?" David turned to glance at her as if he hadn't realized she was across the table from him. That, of course, was absurd. Even the hairs on his arms had been at alert since she sat down.

"Yeah, I do," replied David hesitantly. "You want to go to the beach for a week? I can't pay you, but I'll cover the hotel and all the beer and pizza you can eat! You can share a room with Becky."

Becky was the annoyingly adorable blonde undergrad at the other end of the table dominating the attention of the majority of the men in the room. Leah liked Becky well enough. She was smart and funny and more importantly, she pulled her weight in the studio. But Leah also envied her ease with men. She absorbed the attention of every man in her wake like a sponge, without even trying. Becky could have any guy she wanted with the snap of a finger. Leah's jealousy of the perky blonde had always been a stumbling block to developing a friendship.

"Sounds good. When do we leave?"

David and Leah spent the next half hour heads bent together talking through his plans for the following week. As part of his graduate thesis, David was producing a video about beach regeneration for an environmental group. According to the group, beaches naturally disappeared over time. Tides, time, and storms moved the sand from one beach and deposited it further down the coast. While this was an entirely natural process, homeowners did not appreciate their beaches disappearing and went to extraordinary lengths to prevent it. Barriers, jetties, and seawalls were just a few of the ways that homeowners tried to prevent their pieces of beach from washing downstream. Sand renourishment was a last-ditch attempt to maintain a beachfront by trucking in sand from other places. Coastal environmentalist groups rallied against the process because it destroyed habitats, changed the chemistry of the beach, and the big machinery involved polluted and damaged the area. David had been hired to produce an anti-beach regeneration video to be aired on the area public television station.

The majority of the crew would be local professionals. In fact, she and Becky would be the only non-professionals. She wondered, with a flare of jealousy, what Becky's role was. The floor manager had the glamorous job of counting down the talent—"three, two, one, action!" But in reality, she was only the director's mouthpiece. Floor managers served as the communication link between the production people and the talent, but they also rounded up cold drinks, towels, chairs, and anything else anyone on set needed. In reality, the job was more like a cross between a secretary, errand boy, and circus ringleader.

Catching up with Leah as she walked back to campus, Becky asked, "So . . . what's the scoop with you and Professor McCutie?"

Feeling embarrassment growing in her face, Leah choked out, "What do you mean?"

"You know exactly what I mean! David Leitner—aka—Professor McCutie!" Becky teased.

"I don't know what you are talking about!"

"Yeah right. Whatever. I've seen the way he looks at you when you are not watching." Becky smirked.

Curiosity overriding her discretion, Leah asked, "What do you mean?"

"He looks like a man that hasn't eaten in a while and you are a juicy steak, if you know what I mean!"

"Well . . . he is kinda yummy, isn't he?"

"No shit! Did you see him in those white jeans the other day?" Becky squealed. "I thought I'd have an orgasm just looking at him. But wait, I thought you and Eric were . . . you know . . . a thing!"

Leah felt a familiar pain at the mention of her friend. She had missed his physical presence since he had left for camp at the end of the term. She had also missed their emotional closeness since she had confessed that she didn't love him at the dance.

"No, Eric and I are just friends."

"So . . . are you calling dibs on Professor McCutie?" Becky asked.

Leah nodded. Deciding it would be nice to have someone to talk to about David, she grinned and added, "Yeah, I guess I'm calling dibs."

On the long drive to the coast, Leah concluded that she had misjudged Becky. In addition to her looks, Becky was clever and funny. She knew she was pretty and that men paid attention to her, but she was so self-deprecating that Leah couldn't help but like her. She and Leah found they had a great deal in common besides their taste in men. They shared a bawdy sense of humor. Working with an all-male crew, innuendo and double entendres were as rampant as the booze that flowed after work every evening.

The first night on the coast, she and Becky had discovered that, in addition to tequila shots, men were completely turned on by the girls toking on cigars. Free from judging girlfriends, several of guys had pulled out Cubans after dinner as they sat around the pool. Becky pulled Leah down next to her on a chaise lounge as she asked one of the men if she could try the cigar. Soon the two girls were surrounded by young men offering advice on how best to enjoy the cigar. While Leah didn't particularly enjoy the cigars, she decided the symbolism was pretty obvious.

She had hoped that she and David would continue their game of cat and mouse on this trip, but they were never alone. The crew worked like mules all day and partied into the wee hours every night. David was busy. He had given a few mischievous grins, but there was no privacy or time for flirtation. He often worked late in his hotel room planning the following day's shoot. When David wasn't working, he was part of the gang. Leah had to confess that she was impressed with his ability to direct the rowdy crew during business hours and drink beer and laugh with them later.

Some of the guys had girlfriends, and one even had a

wife, that showed up late in the evening to corral their boozy significant others. The remaining single guys vied for Becky's and Leah's attention hoping for a hook-up. While she enjoyed the attention, Leah had left them all panting.

"You really ought to get you some!" Becky suggested one night as they wandered back to their hotel room.

"What?"

"How about that cutie, Simon? I bet he's got skills."

"I am . . . I'm doing just . . . I . . ." Leah stumbled.

"I just mean, that if you are not going to make a move on you know who, you really ought to partake of the offerings. If you know what I mean?" Leah snorted in laughter as Becky drunkenly wiggled her eyebrows up and down.

"This bush knows what you mean!"

"Speaking of bushes . . ." Becky snorted as she gulped her beer.

"God. You are too much!"

"Yeah, that's what he said!" Becky snickered.

"Which *he*?"

"Doesn't matter. All of 'em!" Becky announced as she struggled to scan the key card and open the door without dropping her beer.

"Jeez, Beck. Here, let me get the door."

"I'm going to," Becky said.

"Going to what?"

"Going to partake. Tomorrow night! You think you could find other accommodations? You know, if I lure poor young Simon to our lair?" By the time Leah had formulated an answer, Becky was face down on her bed passed out.

Leah hadn't given any further thought to Becky's plan until she retreated to her room the following evening. One of Leah's crew socks had been placed over the doorknob. Leah was sure there was a condom joke there somewhere, but in the meantime she was homeless. The night was mild and there was still noises coming from the pool, so Leah decided to rejoin the party.

"Leah! Come on in! The water's great!" Derrick, the tall, attractive Jamaican cameraman announced.

"Nah! I'm tired. I'm just going to hang out a while."

"Why not go on to bed?" Derrick laughed as he swam to the edge of the pool. Glancing around as if counting heads, he laughed. "Oh, never mind, I get it! A tie on the door?"

"A sock!"

Sputtering with laughter, Derrick asked, "Who?"

"Simon, I think. At least that was the plan last night."

"Oh really? My money was on Rafe!"

"What do you mean?" Leah stretched out on her stomach on the chaise lounge so that she could talk to Derrick.

"You know, the sound guy, big, muscular, and macho. I would think that she would go for his type."

"Tonight, I think Simon is her type."

"And what type is that?" Derrick asked.

"Male and willing!"

"You know if you want, I've got an extra bed in my room," Derrick offered.

Leah was not quite sure what Derrick was offering, but judging by the twinkle in his eye, she concluded that she would be safer sleeping on the pool lounger.

"That's sweet, Derrick," Leah demurred innocently, "but I think I'll pass."

Noticing Leah wrapping a towel over her shoulders, he offered, "You sure? I could keep you warm."

"I think she gave you an answer!" a voice from the gate barked. David strode onto the pool deck and gave Derrick a *piss off* look.

Taking the hint, Derrick raised both hands as if in surrender and murmured, "It's cool, man. No offense." He pushed off the side of the pool into a backstroke and swam toward the opposite side of the pool.

"He was just being nice," Leah said a little indignantly.

"No," David said, running a hand roughly through his hair, "he was trying to get into your pants."

"Takes one to know one!" Leah replied without thinking.

After a beat, David burst out laughing. "You really are impossible!" Gesturing at the pool deck, he asked, "So what are you doing out here alone?"

After explaining that her roommate was otherwise occupied, Leah shrugged and sighed. "So I just thought I would hang out here a while."

"You can't sleep out here. It's not safe. Come on. You can stay in my room. I can't have you asleep on your feet tomorrow."

"That doesn't sound very safe either!"

"Don't worry, your virtue's safe with me! I've still got a ton of work to do. I was just out for a walk to clear my head for a minute."

As David reached out to help Leah extricate herself from the pool lounger, the timer on the pool light suddenly thrust them into darkness. David hadn't seen Derrick leave, but they were now alone and in the dark. David was grateful for the darkness so that she could not see how his body responded to her nearness. He had done his best to stay away from her. He had avoided being alone with her. But damn, a man could only handle so much. When he had stumbled upon Derrick flirting with her, a surge of jealousy and protectiveness had shot through him like a spear. Could he really have her alone in his room and keep his hands off? He wanted to touch her so badly that it was physically painful. And worse, she had no inclinations to resist him. He knew that if he kissed her again, a fire would be lit that could not be extinguished.

David mustered the last of his resistance. "Hey, I've got a better idea. Pancakes."

"Pancakes?"

"Yeah, pancakes. There is a Pancake House just a block from here and I've got a craving for pancakes."

"So now you're hungry? I thought you had tons of work to do."

Oh, I am hungry all right, just not for pancakes. But aloud he said, "I'll do the work later, but right now I want to eat pancakes with you." David kicked himself mentally as his mind strayed to what he really wanted to eat.

Pancakes and coffee. Strong black coffee. That was what he needed to keep his mind of this tempting young woman in front of him.

The pancakes were so melt-in-your-mouth delicious that it almost distracted him.

"You know what I love about Pancake House?" Leah asked around a mouthful of pancake.

"Syrup?"

"How did you know?"

David laughed, gesturing to her plate of pancakes swimming in an absurd amount of maple syrup.

"But not just any syrup . . . hot maple syrup. Do you know that you cannot get hot syrup in most restaurants? They say that they don't have a way to heat it, but I think they are just lazy. They don't want to fool with it. That's why I only eat pancakes at Pancake House. That, and the fact that it goes along with my restaurant law."

"And what, pray tell, is you restaurant law?"

Ignoring his shit-eating grin, she replied, "Never order anything in a restaurant if it isn't in the name of the place. For instance, Pancake House, so you order pancakes, or at the Meridian Steakhouse, you order steak, of course."

"That sounds like a reasonable rule. But, what do you order at somewhere like, say, Shafer's?"

Without missing a beat, she deadpanned, "Strawberry pie—duh!"

Before they knew it, the sky was lightning and the tables around them were filling with early risers. "Oh crap, we talked all night. What about all your work?"

Shrugging as he dropped a few bills on the table, David said, "Don't worry about it. I'll manage." Heedlessly he continued, "I'll tell you what. In repayment for making me a terrible director and probably a real grouch today, you can have dinner with me tonight."

"But I thought . . ."

"Don't—It's just dinner. I really enjoyed your company, and I would like to take you somewhere nice tonight."

His heart was not the only thing that leaped when she said yes.

Keep it in your pants, man. She is almost half your age and a student.

But a little voice nudged him and pointed out, *but she is not your student anymore.*

"So . . . how was Simon?" Leah drawled when she and Becky stood sharing the bathroom mirror.

"Positively delish!" Becky gushed.

"Are you going to see him again?"

"I don't know. Maybe. But there's a whole buffet out there. How can I know I like the chicken salad until I've tried the pimento cheese, and the chicken fingers, and the cheese dip, and the . . ."

"And the dill pickles . . ." Leah said, nudging Becky's shoulder.

"Ugh! Gross!"

Leah choked on her toothpaste when Becky added, "Besides, it was more of a gherkin!"

"Where did you get to last night? I looked for you when Simon left, but I figured you had finally taken my advice."

Avoiding Becky's direct gaze, Leah mumbled, "I hung out at the pool awhile."

"And?" Becky encouraged with a rolling motion of her hand.

"And . . . Derrick hit on me."

"Derrick is the tall one with the yummy accent, right? So did you . . . you know . . . play Chitty Chitty Bang Bang?"

"Hey, gross! You are defiling a fond childhood memory!"

"Yeah, whatever! Give me the scoop. Did you and Derrick . . . have sexual relations?" She stage-whispered the last as if she was saying something really nasty.

"Nope, I had pancakes." After a dramatic pause, she added, "With David," and then she strolled out of the room, leaving her friend gaping behind her.

CHAPTER EIGHT: DINNER

The day's shoot had not gone well. Ironically, it was not David's lack of preparation or sleep that had caused the difficulties. Rick, the on-air talent, had food poisoning and kept ruining takes by rushing off set to be sick. By mid-afternoon, David decided to surrender to fate and canceled the rest of the day.

David and Leah worked in companionable silence to shut down the control room. "Hey, can we have an early dinner? I really want to take advantage of the evening to do some rough editing,"

"Sure. No problem. How early?"

"Well . . . I was kind of thinking right now," David said sheepishly.

"That would be more like lunch, but sure. We can get the early bird specials."

"Are you implying that I am old enough to qualify for the senior discount?" David asked, feigning indignation. He snorted in laughter when Leah came back with, "Maybe I can save you a few bucks and get the kid's meal!"

David had tried to convince himself that it just made sense to grab something to eat now. He really did need some time to review his rough footage. They would grab a bite to eat and then he could hide in his room and work through the evening. But the truth was that he couldn't wait to spend more time with her. Impressions of her had been in his head all day—the way she tilted her head back when she laughed, the way she tucked her feet up under her in the booth, the way she slid the empty sugar packets under a placemat so that no one could tell how many sugars she had stirred into her coffee. Six, by the way, she had stirred six sugars into her coffee.

Pulling himself away from his thoughts, David asked, "What are you hungry for?" Catching her greedy gaze, David tilted her chin up and laughed. "Hey, my eyes are up here!"

Leah boldly grinned and offered, "You pick. I am up for anything you want."

It was David's turn to have difficulty swallowing. She was . . . what? Clever? Funny? Beautiful? Tempting? All of the above? Every minute he spent with her was like swimming in water over his head. He could feel himself drowning, but he couldn't bear to get out of the water.

"How about Chinese? I saw a place just down the road."

Bending at the waist with her palms pressed together, Leah aped, "Ah so, you like-y fried lice?" Noticing the baffled look on David's face, she deadpanned, "Yes, Chinese would be fine."

David knew that Leah had been teasing about the early bird special but was amused to find the restaurant vacant except for a few elderly couples. The restaurant felt intimate as they slid into an empty banquette.

"Do you know what you want?" asked David, quickly adding "On the menu!" without looking up.

Covering a laugh, Leah said, "I like Chinese, but I always get the same things. I'd like to try something different. What are you going to have?"

After some discussion, David selected several dishes for the two of them to share. When the waitress placed the dishes in front of them, Leah reached for her silverware but hesitated when she heard David ask for two sets of chopsticks.

"I've never eaten with chopsticks."

"Chinese food is meant to be eaten with chopsticks." Reaching for her hand, David attempted to position the chopstick in her left hand correctly. "Here. Let me show you."

After a hilarious chain of events that ended in several pieces of fried pork flying across the table, Leah managed to move a few small bites to her mouth with the chopsticks.

"No wonder Chinese people are thin!" Leah huffed as she struggled to pick up a dumpling with the wooden sticks. David shot out a hand to catch the doomed dumpling as her pincer grip slipped halfway to her mouth.

"Here." He laughed, bringing the dumpling to her lips. As he slid the dumpling into her mouth, his finger lingered on her lower lip. Leah's eyes involuntarily widened and closed as he traced her bottom lip.

"You are . . . irresistible."

"So . . . stop . . . resisting."

Leah could hear her heartbeat pulsing in her ears. She opened her eyes to see David's green eyes gazing at her. He looked hopelessly lost. She knew he was struggling with his own conscience. There was a war in his eyes between logic and lust. She knew that the tide would turn if she touched him. She almost felt guilty. Almost.

Slowly, without breaking his gaze, she raised her hand to his face. Barely touching him, she drew the backs of her fingers along his jaw. The stubble on his cheeks sent a frisson of pleasure through her.

"Do you want to get out of here?" he croaked.

"Mhmm," was all that Leah could answer.

Grabbing her hand and tossing a few bills on the table, David pulled her from the booth and led her to the front of the restaurant. Behind them, the waitress offered, "Do you want your fortune cookies?"

With a lascivious smile at David, she said sotto voce, "No, he's got all the luck he needs."

Outside the restaurant, David pulled her to the side of the building. "God, I want you," he murmured as he lowered his mouth to hers. "I've tried to do the right thing," he swore as he placed small hot kisses along her neck.

Leah empathized by moaning, "I want you . . . inside me."

David seemed to rein in his spiraling desire long enough to look into her eyes. "Are you sure? If we go much further, I am not going to be able to stop."

Leah responded by reaching between them and running a finger along the outline of his cock straining against his jeans. David gasped and grabbed her hand. He looked questioningly into her eyes, giving her one more chance to back out. Leah tilted her chin up and met his gaze. A silent treaty was reached. There was no more need to battle for power. They were no longer opposing forces. The score no longer mattered. They had both won and both lost.

Lacing his fingers in hers, he murmured, "Let's get out of here!"

They didn't speak on the way back to the hotel. They were both too full of feeling to say anything. David finally dropped her hand, when they reached the parking lot of the hotel. "Do you want to come up to my room?" David asked unnecessarily.

"Yes, I think I do. Do you want me to come up?"

"God help me, but yes, I do."

As they headed toward the elevator, David's cell phone rang. David hesitated to answer it but finally relented when it continued to ring. Leah watched as his eyes, full of desire, cleared and his husky voice became strong and clipped. This was important. Important enough to snap him out of his fuck drunk.

"Yeah, I'll be right there!" David promised, thumbing the phone.

"What's wrong?"

"It was not food poisoning. Rick had a heart attack." Rick was the spokesman for the project and the lead on-air talent. In addition, Rick was a close friend of David's from his advertising days. Without Rick, there was no program.

"I'm sorry, but I've got to go down to the hospital."

"Oh my gosh. Is he okay?"

"They've got him stabilized, but he's in the ICU."

"Do you want me to go with you?" Leah offered.

Hesitating a moment, David sighed. "No, you better stay here. I will need you to coordinate with the crew. I don't know what's going to happen, but we may have to cancel the whole shoot."

"Oh, David!"

"Let's not get ahead of ourselves. The most important thing is for me to get down to the hospital to check on Rick. Can you get in touch with everyone and let them know what's going on?" As floor manager, Leah had a complete list of contact numbers for the crew.

"What about the studio time?" she asked, trying to mirror his business-like manner.

"Go ahead and shut down everything for tomorrow. I'll call you and let you know what to do when I know more." Leah watched David walk back toward the parking lot with a mixture of disappointment and worry. She knew it was wrong to be feeling frustrated when poor Rick was in the hospital, but her body couldn't do the same about-face that her brain had done.

As David started out the door, he abruptly turned and strode back to her. Pulling her to him like a corny swashbuckling pirate, he kissed her deeply. The kiss was passionate but controlled. The kiss felt like a promise. Just as abruptly, he released her and dashed out the door. Leah stood swaying, dizzy and breathless, as the door closed behind him. Suddenly aware of her surroundings, she smiled to herself and pushed the elevator button.

Leah found most of the crew around the pool, as usual. After rounding up the few missing members—including Derrick and Becky who were, not surprisingly, together in his room—she explained what had happened. The crew was sympathetic. Production crews were like families—even a short-term crew like this one, bonded over long hours and hard work. There was a discussion of sending flowers, taking up a collection, and so on, but Leah suggested they wait until they had a little more information. After informing them that they had a day off tomorrow, she promised to let them know as soon as she knew anything else and headed to her room to take a much-needed nap. The last two days had been intense.

By dinner time, David had called to cancel the remainder of the shoot. He planned to stay a few more days to make sure Rick made a full recovery, but there would be no way to continue the project. David would have to re-shoot all of the spokesman shots later. Hopefully, they had enough B-roll to complete the program when he found a new spokesman. B-roll was the alternative footage that was intercut with the main video pieces.

Leah worked late into the evening canceling studio time, catering trucks, and arranging for all of the crew to be paid and dismissed. She and Becky decided they would stop by the hospital the following morning on their way out of town. Leah explained the situation to the desk clerk, and he kindly allowed her, with his supervision, to collect a change of clothes for David. She also grabbed his backpack and notes. She'd guessed, correctly, that he was already working on Plan B.

David was asleep in an uncomfortable hospital lounger when Becky and Leah tiptoed into Rick's hospital room the following morning. Leah couldn't help but stare. She had never seen him asleep. She bent down and brushed a small kiss on his lips. A lazy smile creased his face as his eyes fluttered open to see her.

"That's the best wakeup call I've ever had."

"Good morning to you, too," Leah whispered with a mischievous grin. A subtle cough behind her reminded her that Becky still stood in the doorway. Blushing, Leah stood and recited the arrangements she had made the previous evening. "And here, I . . . uhm . . . we . . . brought you a change of clothes and your backpack."

"That was very thoughtful of you, Miss Gwaltney," David said in an attempt to regain his composure.

"Oh please!" Becky groaned. "Like everybody didn't know you two were going to end up together!"

David looked at Becky in surprise, shrugged, and reached out for Leah's hand. "Well, she is irresistible!"

Changing the subject, Leah asked how Rick was doing.

"I would be doing better if there wasn't all this heavy breathing going on in here," Rick grumbled from behind closed eyes. "How's a guy supposed to get any sleep?" He raised and lowered his eyebrows lasciviously to indicate that he was just teasing them.

"Well, you sound just fine," Becky remarked.

"And you look just fine," Rick countered as he opened his eyes to appreciate Becky. Leah could swear that she saw Becky blush.

Interrupting, Leah announced, "Well, I guess we better

get on the road. We just wanted to stop by and see if you needed anything."

"Dave, why don't you walk these ladies down to the elevator?" Rick suggested, but as Leah and David headed out the door, Rick reached out and grabbed Becky's hand. "Stay here. Give them a little privacy. Besides . . . I could use the company." Rick wiggled his eyebrows again implying that he could use more than company.

"I'm sorry," David murmured as they walked toward the elevators.

"For what?"

"For how things worked out. Or I guess didn't work out!" David said, shrugging his shoulders.

"Don't worry about it! We'll just call it foreplay!" Leah teased.

David stopped abruptly and grabbed Leah's shoulders, turning her to face him. "Leah, we can't do this! You know I am more than twice your age!"

Leah felt heat rising in her cheeks. *What is happening here? Is he backing out? I thought we had reached an understanding.* "What are you trying to say?" Leah whispered.

"I'm trying to say that you should be with someone your own age. You deserve more than this broken down old man!"

"What about what I want?"

"You are so young! You don't even know what you want," David insisted, looking miserable.

Leah was embarrassed, hurt, angry, and disappointed. In an attempt to prevent the tears from falling, she tilted her chin up, narrowed her eyes, and said, "How very condescending of you!"

"I'm sorry. I don't mean to be. I'm just trying to make you see that you deserve better than this." David sighed, rubbing a hand across his tired, unshaven face.

Leah's eyes glittering with anger and unshed tears. "And

what about you? Are you old enough to know what you want?"

David hesitated. The truth was that he wanted her and not just physically. The truth was that he was falling in love with her. But the truth was not what she needed to hear right now. "I am ... old enough to know better!" he finally choked out.

David saw the slap coming and didn't bother to dodge it. He figured that he had it coming. He had let this happen. He should have been stronger.

"Go to hell!" she whispered as she turned to find the stairwell. The slap had left his face stinging, but it did not hurt nearly as much as the sight of the door closing behind her.

Noticing the red blooming on his face as David returned to the hospital room, Becky asked, "Oh shit, what did you do to earn that?"

"The right thing!" David insisted irritably.

"I'm not so sure about that! Sure doesn't look like Leah thought it was the right thing!"

David pushed the hospital door open and hinted none too subtly for Becky to leave. "Leah's downstairs."

"Okay, okay, I'm going, but if you hurt my friend ..." Becky began, but when she saw the pain in his eyes, she seemed to relent. Reaching out to touch his stinging face, she murmured, "I hope you made the right choice."

She had left the room before he mumbled, "Yeah, so do I."

Leah pretended to sleep on the trip back to campus so that she did not have to answer any of Becky's questions. Thankfully, Becky seemed to understand that she wasn't ready to talk. When Becky pulled her car up to the dormitory, she hugged Leah and told her, "Call me when you are ready to talk about it." Leah was surprised but nodded morosely.

When she hadn't heard from Leah after a few days, Becky showed up at her dorm and cajoled her into going for coffee. Leah eventually spilled all of the painful details over tall white chocolate mochas and warm blueberry muffins.

"So, what's the plan here?" Becky asked.

"What do you mean plan? I have no plan. I just want to forget David Leitner and move on!" Leah insisted.

"Well . . . that's your plan then. How are you going to accomplish this?"

"I don't have the slightest idea."

Leah did her best to turn off her heart and brain for the rest of the summer. After a week of moping in her dorm room, she decided that Becky was right. She needed a plan. She needed to keep busy. She found the most mindless job she could and spent the rest of the summer scooping ice cream at the Dairy Barn. She worked as many hours as the owner would give her. The owner, an older woman named Sal, suspected there was a man behind Leah's frenzied work ethic, but she minded her own business.

A few weeks after the canceled shoot, Becky showed up at the Dairy Barn and dragged Leah to a late movie. "You know he rescheduled the shoot?" Becky ventured on their walk back to campus.

"What shoot?" Leah asked, attempting nonchalance.

Becky stopped and gave her a look that said, "Give me a break!"

"You know exactly what I am talking about."

"Fine, whatever! I don't care."

"Right . . . I can tell."

Leah had avoided the Telecommunications Department and any chance of running into David. She had dropped the summer classes that were in her major. She had kept the media law class because it met in the Business Annex and there was no chance of running into David there. She had avoided all department social activities. Becky tried to keep her from becoming a complete hermit by forcing her to go out to dinner or a movie occasionally. Otherwise, she worked, and she slept. Vic had called once to ask her to dinner, but she'd given him the brush off. Becky had given her a hard time about that because it had been Becky that had encouraged Vic to call her. But she just wasn't ready. She couldn't even imagine ever being ready again. She'd received a few funny postcards from Eric and one long rambling letter full of funny camp stories. She knew that she should write him back, but she just didn't have the energy.

When David accidentally blundered into the ice cream shop late one evening late near the end of summer, he was a startled as she was. She had pasted on a sickly sweet smile and attempted to serve him as if he was any other customer.

"Leah, how are you?" he began.

"Thanks for coming to Dairy Barn," she said through her false smile. When he attempted to continue to try to engage her, she added, "Is there anything else I can get for you, sir? If not, please excuse me, I have other customers," she said, gesturing to the empty store. With that, Leah strode through the store to the back office. Pulling her apron off and balling it up, she tossed it on Sal's desk and announced, "I quit!" as she escaped through the back of the store.

Leah knew that she was being overly dramatic. She would go back later and apologize to Sal. But in truth, Sal had known she would be leaving when the fall semester began. There was barely any business this close to the end of the summer. The tourists were gone, and the students were not back yet. Scooping ice cream had only been meant to keep her busy and now he had ruined that.

She had known that she was not over him. She could not stop reliving every moment they had spent together. The pleasant memories were almost more painful to recall than the bad ones. But after the first miserable week in the dorm, she had decided that she couldn't continue to torture herself. She devised a strategy to push her painful thoughts to the back burner. Every time her thoughts went to him, she forced herself to sing every verse of "The Star Spangled Banner" inside her head. It worked, but God, she was mightily sick of that song!

David's heart had leaped when he walked into the Dairy Barn and seen Leah. She looked ridiculous and adorable, in her ruffled pink Dairy Barn apron. Her dark red hair was pulled back into a ponytail with an absurdly large pink bow which only served to accentuate her youth. He noticed that she looked too thin and tired. She was not taking good care of herself. With a total lack of arrogance, he knew that was his fault.

The truth was that he was in no better shape. He taught his summer classes. He tried to run or ride his bike, but they were solitary activities that left him too much time to think. He filled every minute he could with work. He had finished his beach reclamation project and would present it to his thesis committee in the fall. The environmentalists were happy with it, so he assumed his committee would be as well. He had driven back to the coast to spend time with Rick as he went through rehab. But, he ate only when he had to and managed to sleep after too many of glasses of wine each night. He had lost weight and felt even older than he looked. He had spent the summer trying to remember, or believe, that he had done the right thing. Most of the time, he succeeded. Seeing Leah again was like ripping off a bandaid. It stung intensely at first and then it started to bleed all over again.

David had not meant for things to go so wrong. He should have stopped this flirtation when it started. If he was honest with himself, he hadn't because it stroked his ego. Not that he was not equally attracted to her, but he was also very flattered that this sexy young thing was attracted to him.

He should have shut it down. He knew from the beginning that he was too old for her and seeing his pal Rick in that hospital bed that night had cooled his ardor like an ice bath. He and Rick were nearly the same age. They were old enough to worry about things like heart attacks and prostate exams, while she should be worrying about what she would wear to the next dance.

He had almost surrendered again when she woke him up with that kiss. Opening his eyes to see her beautiful face smiling down at him was something he could imagine doing for the rest of his life. But she deserved someone her own age, even if she didn't know it. He hadn't meant to be blunt or condescending. He hadn't even known what he was going to say when he started talking. He just jumped in with both feet, and the more he talked, the deeper the hole he dug for himself became. He had betrayed her. She had always been honest and sincere. He was the one that had been deceitful. He was the one that was lying to himself and to her.

He wanted her. He couldn't stop thinking about her. He was in love with her. But he had pushed her away, and he had suffered for it every day since.

CHAPTER NINE: FALL SEMESTER

"You've got to be fucking kidding me!" Leah exclaimed loudly to no one or everyone. The crowd of students registering for classes quieted for a moment at her outburst. A few students looked over at her questioningly. Leah ignored them all. Of all the bad luck! She had been assigned David Leitner as her advisor for her senior project. She would have to get it changed. She would have to!

Leah had been preparing herself for seeing David again. Seeing him at the Dairy Barn had ripped a hole in her heart. The last few weeks had been a struggle. She was certain that she would see him around the department when fall classes began. She might even have to take a class from him again, but she wasn't prepared for this! Seniors were expected to write, produce, and edit a short film to be presented at the end of the year to a jury for evaluation. Each student was assigned an individual advisor. She would have to meet one on one with her advisor throughout the year while she worked on her project. And of all the absurd bad luck, David was her assigned advisor.

As Leah fumed and debated how she could get her advisor changed, she heard Eric shouting across the quad, "Hey! Leah!"

Looking up, she saw his lanky frame bobbing through the crowd to reach her. "Hey! I've been trying to call you," he said. He looked good. His skin was browned from a summer outdoors and his hair fell longer than usual around his ears.

"Sorry. I've been busy," she lied. She knew he had returned to campus the previous week, but she had been avoiding him and ducking his calls.

"Listen, I want you to meet someone." Eric smiled as a lithe brunette with a heart-shaped face and big blue eyes stepped up beside him. "This is Rachel. We met at camp this summer. She is transferring here this semester!"

Leah felt a pang in her chest, not quite jealousy, but loss, when she realized the implication. He had met someone—someone special. She was losing Eric, just like she had lost David. Even though it was not the kind of love he had wanted from her, she knew that she did love Eric in her own way. Now Rachel was going to replace her and Eric would be gone, too.

Straightening, Leah realized that she was being unfair to Eric, again. Eric deserved to be happy. Eric deserved for her to be happy for him! Leah pushed aside her own feelings and smiled at Rachel. "So, Rachel, today is Wednesday and we have a tradition around here . . ."

After her initial misgivings, Leah decided that she actually liked Rachel. Life was about change and her relationship with Eric had changed. Leah knew that she had to adapt to the new situation if she wanted to maintain her friendship with Eric. Rachel was obviously beautiful, but she was also funny and intelligent. Best of all, it was clear that she adored Eric.

When Rachel excused herself to go to the restroom, Eric leaned in and quietly asked, "Hey, are you okay?"

"Yeah, sure."

Eric had been gone all summer. He didn't know how disastrously her summer had turned out. She had done her best to act normal. She had laughed and smiled at all the right places. She had even made a real effort with Rachel.

"I mean, I tried to call you, you know, to give you a heads up about Rachel."

Oh, he was worried about surprising me with Rachel.

Leah was a little disappointed that Eric had not seen through her false gaiety. Not that she would have dumped all her misery on him, but still it stung a little that he didn't notice how unhappy she really was. Reaching across the table to touch his hand, she said, "It's okay, Eric. I want you to be happy. I'm glad you found someone. I like her."

"I'm glad you like her. I am crazy about her." He grinned.

With mock sarcasm, Leah laughed. "No kidding! I couldn't tell."

After too many Bloody Marys at Mother's, Leah excused herself, pointing out that she needed to get to the registrar's office before five. She did not attempt to explain her predicament to the happy pair. Eric and Rachel didn't need to hear about her awkward relationship with David.

Leah reached the registrar's office and stood in line with other disgruntled students wanting to drop, add, or otherwise change their schedules. She reached the grated window as the clock ticked 4:58. Leah, remembering an old adage about flies and honey, smiled at the weary clerk.

"Tough day, huh?" Leah sympathized.

"Don't you know it. So, what can I do for you?"

"I, uhmm, I want to change my senior advisor." She quickly realized the dilemma she was in when the clerk asked the next and obvious question.

"Why?"

After a long pause, Leah asked, "Do I have to give a reason?"

The clerk studied Leah thoughtfully. "Well, sweetie, I have to put something down on the request form. Is there a problem?"

Is there a problem? Leah thought sadly. *Is my heart breaking every time I think about him* a problem? *Is my body on fire every time I touch him* a problem? *Is wanting him so bad that it physically hurts* a problem?

Finally, Leah admitted, "No ma'am, there isn't a problem."

"Well, I can't change your advisor unless you can give me a reason," the clerk explained.

"But I . . ." Leah could not imagine any good way to end that sentence.

"Yes?" the clerk urged.

"Never mind, I've changed my mind. Sorry to have wasted your time," Leah apologized to the clerk as she followed her out of the building. As the clerk locked the door behind her, Leah murmured to herself, "Well damn! Now what?" Apparently, she was going to have to deal with this somehow. Somewhere, deep beneath the Star Spangled Banner, Leah felt a traitorous spark of excitement.

Chapter Ten: Senior Advisor

Leah changed clothes for the third time. "What about this?"

Sprawling on Leah's dorm bed, Becky looked up from the magazine she was flipping through. "Nope, I liked the first one. It showed off your . . . advantages!"

"I don't want to show off my advantages, or whatever!" Leah huffed.

"I call—bullshit!" Becky announced without looking up. "You have been moping around all summer. Now you are going to see David again, thanks to me, and—"

"Whoa! Wait a minute! What do you mean *thanks to you*?" Leah interrupted.

"Well," Becky began apologetically, "you know I am friends with Lori, the Telecomm secretary, and I, uhm, I might have had some influence on who she assigned to you!"

"What?"

"You mean . . . oh Beck, how could you?" Leah flopped onto the other empty twin bed.

"You two need to work this out! You are miserable! He is miserable!"

"He's miserable?" Leah asked momentarily forgetting her anger.

"Yes! He has moped around all summer like his dog died!"

"Well good!" Leah concluded indignantly. "He deserves to be miserable!"

"Well, since we have identified that, in fact, everyone is miserable, let's find you an outfit that will make him really sorry!" Becky suggested.

They finally decided upon a purple V-neck sweater and jeans that were the perfect combination of casual and sexy. The jeans accentuated her curves perfectly and the sweater suggested, more than showed her cleavage. Sexiness, she knew, was sometimes about what you couldn't see as much as what you could see. The outfit made her feel sexy and strong. She needed all the confidence she could muster. She was about to see David alone for the first time in nearly six weeks

Across campus, Rick was also berating David. "So tell me again why you turned down that beautiful young woman?"

"Because, you ass, I am too old for her. She's just a kid. She doesn't know what she wants."

"It sure seemed like she knew what she wanted to me," Rick offered.

"I had to stop things before anybody got hurt!"

"Yeah, I see how well that worked out! You are miserable. She is miserable. Why don't you just call her?"

"I don't have to," David muttered, tossing a sheet of paper listing his assigned advisees across the table to Eric.

Eric skimmed down the page until he reached Leah's name. Letting out a small whistle, he asked, "So, what are you going to do?"

"I haven't the slightest idea!" David concluded miserably.

David, securely ensconced behind his desk, looked up when Leah knocked on the frame of the open door. He had dreaded this moment from the minute he saw his list of advisees. He knew how difficult this was going to be for both of them. He had thought a lot about how to make this easier. All of this was his fault and he knew that.

David cleared his throat and began, "Hi."

"I tried to get my advisor changed," Leah blurted. He saw her cheeks flush with color and realized she had not intended to tell him that.

"Oh," he replied lamely. David felt stung by her admission.

After an awkward moment of silence, David gestured toward a chair. "Do you want to come in?"

Leah's gaze flew to his. David immediately recognized his mistake, recalling the last time he had asked her into a room. "Please, have a seat." Leah perched on the edge of the chair like a bird ready to take flight at the slightest provocation.

"So . . . how are you?" David asked tentatively.

The glittering tears that filled her eyes answered his question. Damn! He was making this worse. He needed to take control and make this right for her. Deciding to change tacks, he began, "Okay, I guess this first meeting is just to explain the expectations for your project. We need to set up a schedule of benchmarks where we will meet and assess your progress."

Leah cleared her throat and nodded for him to continue. After a half hour, they had mapped out a plan for her project. The tension was still there like static electricity, but neither of them acknowledged it. His body ached for her touch and it was all the more painful because he knew the touch would never come. *Maybe, if we keep it all business, we could get through this.*

It only took an accidental brush of her hand to disabuse him of this hope. They reached for the same ink pen and their hands had touched, sending electric shocks through them both. They froze—their fingers barely touching. David felt like all of the air had been sucked out of the room. Neither of them spoke. He couldn't bear to move.

At last, Leah cleared her throat. "I guess that is enough for today." David was both grateful and furious that she'd broken the spell.

"Yes, well . . ." Leah began gathering her things to leave. "I'll have a couple of ideas roughed out for next week."

David stood as she turned toward the door. "I . . ." he began. Leah stopped, her back to him, and waited for him to continue. "I . . . guess I'll see you next week." Leah's shoulders dropped as she walked out of his office without another word.

David stood and stared after her for a long time. He wanted to stop her. He wanted to pull her into his arms and kiss her until she forgot all her pain. He wanted to bend her over his desk and fuck her until he forgot his own pain. An uncomfortable fullness in his jeans reminded him that this was not a productive train of thought.

Too many nights his traitorous cock had woken him up from dreams about Leah. Sliding his hand up and down his own shaft had given him release, but not comfort. Jerking himself off had only accentuated the loneliness and loss he felt without her. What had he been thinking! What had he intended to say to her? His mind swirled with the possibilities. *I'm sorry?* No. He was certain she did not want to hear apologies. *Let me explain?* Again, he doubted she would listen and what could he really say that would make this any better? His thoughts glanced off an idea in the back of his mind. He tried to avoid it, but it kept shoving its way to the front. *What if? What if I had said . . . I love you?*

Leah walked through the gathering evening allowing all her pain and anger to pour out of her with her tears. There wouldn't be enough verses of The Star Spangled Banner in the world to tonight.

"Shit! Shit! Shit!" she muttered through clenched teeth.

What did I expect? He dumped me, remember that! The humiliation and pain of it washed over her anew. *Why do I even care? He is just a good-looking guy that I want to fuck. Nothing more!* Snorting in derisive laughter through her tears, she thought, *he probably has a really tiny dick.*

Looking up, she realized that she had walked to Becky's apartment. Upon seeing Leah's face, Becky immediately remarked, "Oh, honey, come on in. You need a drink!" A bottle and a half of cheap wine later, Leah had passed from tears to rage and back to tears. The alcohol was finally beginning to numb her pain.

Struggling drunkenly to sit up from her beanbag chair, Becky asked, "Let me ask you something?"

"Hmm?"

"Why do you care? There are plenty of other guys out there. You could have your pick! Why do you care what that asshole Leitner thinks or does?"

"Because I . . ." Leah began.

"Say it!" Becky demanded. "I know it. You know it. Just say it!"

"Fine! Because I am in love with him!" Leah finally admitted. "Oh shit, Beck! I am. I am in love with him." Briefly, Leah's faced lit with joy at the realization, but it soon clouded with tears as she wailed, "Shit, Becky! That just makes it worse!"

Leah finally cried and drank herself to sleep. She awoke the next morning slumped on Becky's couch. Her mouth tasted like a gym sock and her eyelids felt like they were made of sandpaper.

"Good morning, sunshine!" a perky blonde Becky chirped from the kitchen doorway. "Come on, get up. I've made breakfast."

"Ugh! I don't want anything to eat," Leah moaned.

"You need to get something in your stomach. It'll give you something to throw up later. Dry heaves suck!"

In too much pain to argue, Leah stumbled into the kitchen. Two plates of scrambled eggs and dry toast were on the table. Two aspirin were sitting on a napkin next to her plate. "And now the real cure for a hangover—a fresh fountain soda! I don't know why but the carbonation always helps! I ran down to the gas station to get it while you were snoring!"

"I don't snore!" Taking a sip of the fizzy drink, she added, "And thanks. You are a good friend."

"It's just soda, you don't have to get all mushy about it, and yes, you do snore."

"You know what I mean," Leah corrected. Without waiting for a response, she added, "And now where is your bathroom? I think I'm going to be sick!"

By lunch, Leah was feeling human again. "God, you are such a light-weight!" Becky said.

"Yeah, but it makes me a cheap date!" Leah laughed.

"Cheap, my ass. That wine cost me thirty bucks."

"A bottle?" Leah asked incredulously.

"No, a case!" Becky laughed uproariously. Finally wiping tears of laughter from her face, Becky said, "But seriously . . ."

"I'll get you some more wine!"

"I'm not talking about the wine. I don't care about the stupid wine! I care about you."

"Awww, now who's getting all mushy?"

"Lee, I'm serious. You've got to do something about David."

"I don't want to talk about this," Leah interrupted.

"Good! Don't talk. Just listen. You've got to do something. You are eating yourself up. I can't stand seeing you like this. I thought forcing you two together would help, but judging by last night—it did not! *Mea Culpa!*"

"The way I see it, you have three choices." Becky ticked them off on her fingers. "One, move on—which you are clearly not doing. Two, tell him that you love him and see what happens or three—" she paused dramatically "—get him to admit that he is in love with you."

Leah looked up at her friend. "I think he proved that he is definitely not in love with me. What makes you think he is in love with me?"

"Seriously? Of course he is!"

Leah tried to squelch the stirring of hope in her chest. "But, he dumped me."

"Sweetie, if he wasn't in love, he would have just fucked you and walked away. No harm, no foul! He sent you packing to protect you! I guarantee he was thinking *I'm this old geezer and she should be with some young stud.*"

"He did say something like that," Leah began.

"Besides, I talked to Rick and he agrees with me. He thinks David saw him in the hospital and it freaked him out."

"Wait a minute. When did you talk to Rick?"

"Well . . . we've sort of been seeing each other," Becky confessed sheepishly.

"Since when? Why didn't you tell me? Why didn't you say anything?"

"Since the week he got out of the hospital, and well, sweetie, you've been a little self-absorbed this summer."

"Oh, Beck, I'm sorry. I've just been . . ." Leah apologized.

"Don't worry about it. I'm not judging. I just didn't feel like you wanted to hear about my love life. Anyway, back to you. Rick and I are sure that David is in love with you. He's just hung up on the age thing. He thinks you are too young to know what you want. You've just got to get him to believe that you know what you want and realize he cannot live without you."

"And how exactly am I going to do that?"

"Trust me! I've got an idea. And, well, let's just say this plan is a win-win," Becky promised with a conspiratorial grin.

Chapter Eleven: Black Op

Leah spent the next week planning her assault. That's how she thought of it, as a military maneuver—a full on black op. She would go for broke—play all her cards at once. Becky was right. What did she have to lose? If he was really in love with her, she would win him over. If he wasn't, well, she couldn't feel any worse, could she?

Leah braced herself as she entered Studio Five and headed toward David's office. *Good, the room is full of impressionable young freshmen.* Although her original appointment had been for late in the afternoon, she had called and rescheduled for midday when she knew the studio would be full of students. For her plan to work, she needed David to be trapped in his office. She needed his undivided attention, and she needed to take control.

"Well, here goes nothing!" Leah said under her breath. Leah lifted her chin and strode confidently to the door of David's office. "Hey, thanks for meeting with me now," she said breezily as he waved her in. Closing the door behind her, she leaned back against it and surreptitiously pushed in the locking mechanism. She wanted him trapped in here, but she also wanted to make sure the throng of students stayed on the other side of the door!

Leah continued to lean against the door and waited. She had to get him on her side of the desk. She knew that he was using that desk as a blockade to prevent her from getting too close. A smile twitched her lips as she remembered how she and Becky had schemed to get him out from behind his barrier. Each scenario had grown more and more outrageous and ridiculous until they were rolling on the floor in fits of laughter.

Leah stilled her face and stood, eyes cast down, waiting for David. The silence grew heavy. Leah peeked through her lashes to see that David was watching her.

"Leah? Is everything okay?"

Wait. Wait. Wait. Let him come to you. Leah held her breath.

When Leah refused to look up or answer him, he did exactly what they had planned. He stood up and moved to her side of the desk. Tentatively, he reached out and lifted her chin. "Leah, talk to me!"

When he saw the tears shimmering in her eyes, he pleaded, "Oh God, Leah. I'm so sorry. I never meant to . . ." He looked like his soul had been ripped open and she knew that this was her opening.

With one finger across his lips, she silenced him. Locking her gaze with his, she slid her finger across his lips. She watched in triumph as his pupils dilated when he recognized the sweet smell of sex on her finger. His gaze flew to hers questioningly. His lips parted with a sigh as he darted his tongue out to taste her sweetness. He couldn't seem to resist as he drew her finger into his mouth. She saw a smug grin on his face when she let out the breath she had been holding. *Oh, no you don't, buddy boy. I am in charge here!*"

Slowly she drew her finger from his mouth and trailed it down his chest, stopping at his waistband. With a wicked glint in her eyes, she slid her hand from him to her own crotch. He watched as she eased up her very short skirt and slid her finger under the damp lacy triangle.

She allowed her head to fall back and closed her eyes as she fingered herself for him.

"Jesus," he whispered, reaching for her. She allowed him to briefly feel how soft and warm and wet she was before pushing his hand away and shaking her head like he was a naughty schoolboy.

"Leah . . ." he began. She silenced him again with her wet fingers. Tilting her head, she reminded him that there was a room full of naive young students on the other side of the door.

He pulled her to him and kissed her desperately, deeply. She surrendered to the hum of her body, allowing him to possess her for just a moment. Then she pulled away from his kiss, leaving him aching for more.

Leah nudged him until he was backed into the edge of the desk. *Hah, right where I want you!* Staring defiantly into his eyes, she slid her hands down his body, stopping again at his waistband. Nimbly but excruciatingly slowly, she worked the buttons on his button fly jeans. Each one popped free relieving a small measure of pressure in his crotch. As the last button slid loose, she eased his jeans down so that he stood, ridiculously, in a puddle of denim, his boxers tented absurdly by his straining cock.

He ached so badly for her to touch him that he could feel himself trembling. He could never get enough of her. He could spend his life drinking her in and still die of thirst.

Finally breaking her gaze, he sucked in his breath and threw back his head to savor the sensation as she drew a finger along his aching erection. He was not fighting her anymore. He wanted her and he couldn't have stopped now if his life depended upon it. Sensing her gaze, he raised his head and looked into her eyes. He loved her. He knew it with earth-shattering certainty. He would tell her. He couldn't deny her any longer.

He opened his mouth to confess but was struck speechless when she slid her hand into his boxers and pulled his cock free. Using her other hand to slide his boxers to the ground, she lowered herself to her knees. Slowly she stroked the length of him. Cupping his balls in her other hand, she squeezed lightly. She used her thumb to slide the pre-cum over the tip of his cock. Just when he thought he would surely die from the pure pleasure of her touch, he felt her drag her tongue along his shaft. Reaching the tip, she opened her lips and enveloped him with her hot wet mouth.

As she moved her mouth up and down on his erection, he began to moan. Every time she heard him make a sound, she would stop and cast her eyes up at him. The sight of her on her knees, with his cock buried in her mouth, was almost more than he could bear, but he understood. They could not make any noise. His office barely had walls and there was a room full of people on the other side of his door. The slightest noise would give them away.

While he knew this was dangerous, it was also intoxicating. When he could not bear it another moment, he reached down to still her head from it rhythmic bobbing. He pulled her to her feet and kissed her, tasting himself on her lips. Reaching down to her hips, he slid her skirt up and moved his hand between her legs. Pushing aside her damp panties, he slid his finger along her wet crease. When his thumb caressed her clit, she gasped. He stopped and looked down at her, smirking. He was playing her game now. If he couldn't make any noise, neither could she. When he eased his finger into her, she bit her lip to keep from crying out. He worked her with his fingers and thumb until she rocked against his hand greedily.

When he heard her whisper, "Oh God, please," he shifted so that he was sitting bare-assed on his desk. Lifting her onto his lap, he positioned her so that she straddled him. She raised to her knees to allow him to position himself and then she slid down onto him. The sensation sent them both reeling. She paused, breathless, to look into his eyes. He was as lost as she was.

David struggled to focus. He needed to tell her. Now. Before. But he could barely think, much less speak. When she paused, he finally found his voice. "I am in love with you."

"I know." She smiled.

"What do you . . ." he began, but he was unable to finish his thought as she began to move, sending them both to the edge of silent hedonistic madness.

Later as they trembled, sweat-drenched in each other's arms, David was finally able to finish his question. "What do you mean, you know? I confess my undying love and you say I know! Seriously, Leah, that's cold!" David teased.

"Lighten up, Leitner, you had that coming." She raised her head to look directly into his soft green eyes. "Besides, you know I am in love with you, too."

David reached up to stroke her face and lowered his mouth to kiss her gently. Leah could feel his erection growing hard again beneath her.

"Jeez, David, I thought you were too old to be this horny. I figured you'd need a nap at least!" Leah smirked.

"You, my dear, are a smartass! And I may just have to spank you for it," David replied with a delicious twinkle in his eye.

The knock on the door startled both of them out of their banter.

"Dave? Hey, Dave, it's Rick. Becky asked me to come check on you. Is everything okay?"

"Uhm, Rick, I am . . ." David stumbled, peering around at the bits of discarded clothing slung around the room and the pile of scripts that had been unceremoniously shoved off the desk.

Leah slapped her hand across her mouth but was too late to stifle her giggles.

"Leah? Is that you?" Rick asked through the door.

After a pause, Leah replied, "Yes, and David cannot come out to play right now!"

"Well, I guess I can tell Beck that you guys worked things out!" Rick laughed and then added, "When you two come up for air, call us and we'll grab some dinner."

Looking into Leah's eyes, David replied, "Better make it breakfast, tomorrow, Pancake House. My girl really loves pancakes!" With his eyes shining with love, he kissed the most beautiful co-ed he had ever seen and the woman he loved.

YOU MAY ALSO ENJOY THE FOLLOWING FROM EXTASY BOOKS INC:

A Time to Dance
Jojo Brown

Excerpt

From where she stood on the balcony of her seventh-story apartment, she knew that with the slightest glance he would be able to see right through the thin cotton blouse she had on. That was the whole idea though, wasn't it?

She wanted him to look, wanted him to see her, wanted to distract him — even if just for a moment. After all, he had distracted her for well over a week now and Celeste figured it was time for a little pay back.

At thirty-two years of age, Celeste had come to the point in her life where she was very happy and content with the way most of it was going. The ability to write was her passion for as long as she could remember. Her mother would tell you — if she were in one of her seldom kind moods — Celeste had been born with a pencil in her hand and a vivid imagination.

Straight out of college she got a good job at the international trades firm owned by a friend of her father. Everyone felt, except Celeste, that with her natural flare with words, she should be happy and content with her position.

To the horror of her parents, she had walked away from it four years ago. Since then, she'd happily written romances and she truly felt that it was the perfect job for her. It was much better than a stuffy office with proposals and reports for things she didn't really care about to write.

Now she made her living softly wrapped in the whites and creams of her airy apartment. She was her own time manager, deadline keeper and more importantly—her own supervisor. Of course, her editor gave her the main deadlines, but within that time frame Celeste was in control of everything.

She loved her job, her apartment and, until recently, her neighbourhood. When they first saw the renovated office building in the city's core, her family was obscenely concerned. To begin with, they didn't like the idea of her living alone in the city.

Even on the day that she moved in, her mother tried to convince her to go back to her office job and live in the cramped box with tight security, within easy reach of her constant advice.

Oh yes—her mother had always been a vault of good advice. Everything from what kind of schools to attend to whom she should date, had come under the heading of mother knows best, until the day Celeste moved into the city.

Mother simply could not understand why Celeste felt the need to escape the corporate world, nor could she see the sense in moving away from her own class.

The family's class was so ridiculously over and above most of the people she dealt with, it was as if they were from a different universe. She came from old money, born with the proverbial silver spoon balanced between her pink lips. She'd grown up in a vast house filled with butlers, chauffeurs, maids and nannies and had always bristled against the expectations of her parents.

They felt she needed to marry well. In other words, a man handpicked by them. Then they expected her to keep a good home, lord herself over her own army of servants. The only work expected of her would be to help with whatever good cause run by the Ladies Auxiliary of the Country Club at the time.

Celeste couldn't stand it anymore. She needed to spread her wings, become her own person and desperately needed to put some mileage, between her and her overbearing parents. They had not forgiven her yet, perhaps they never would.

Her apartment had been just the ticket with its large windows, open floor plan and fantastic view. She quickly settled into the life she'd always dreamed of. Her favourite place was out on the balcony. From there, she looked over the top of any building around and marvelled in the beauty of the lazy, dark river running through the centre of the city. At least it was, until very recently.

When the construction started in the empty lot next to Celeste's building, she was sorely unimpressed. The noise alone was enough to drive any sane person to the nut house. Then of course, as the heavy machines rumbled in and out all day, the quietly eclectic neighbourhood had lost most of its appeal.

Until this, she had always relished her time at the computer beside an open window. The fresh breeze on a spring day or the sound of light summer rain always helped take her mind away from the city, from the sometimes-harsh reality of life. For a writer, the ability to escape the confines of reality is almost as important as air.

She kept the window shut tight, since to have it open even the smallest crack would be to invite a torrent of dust and unpleasant odours into her sanctuary.

The assault carried on for more weeks than she cared to remember. She tried sleeping through the day in order to write in the quiet hours of the night. Forget that. To get any proper rest when the very building shuddered from the force exerted so near its foundations was impossible.

She tried to take her laptop and head out each morning to a park or a coffee shop. Then spend the day tucked away in a back booth, sipped coffees and nibbled on whichever pastry struck her fancy while her fingers tapped furiously away at the keyboard.

The few customers that drifted in and out, acted as a wonderfully calming background noise for her efforts. It was sort of fun. No one noticed her as she sat quietly and watched the ordinary lives of everyday people. It all worked superbly—for a while. Then the schools let out for summer break and it became impossible to find a spot in the city without noisy distractions.

After one final attempt to find solitude within the urban jungle, Celeste solemnly slunk back to her not so quiet corner of the world. Her idea to hide in the shade of an ancient maple tree in the back corner of a local park had gone the way of the dinosaurs. Six rather rambunctious, loud teenaged boys armed with a Frisbee had laid claim to that corner of the park.

To her amazement, the ugly iron monster had grown to great heights without her notice. It stood majestically above the plywood walls, which surrounded its base. As she approached this unwelcome intruder in her world, catcalls and obscenities assaulted Celeste's ears.

The men who scurried around upon the skeleton of the creature they helped bring to life gave it a voice. Not only was it ugly and messy, it was rude and obnoxious.

After that day, just going out to the shops became a chore, one she put off as much as she could.

Celeste began to pray for rain as this would keep the animals at bay. The site would be blessedly quiet, other than the patter of raindrops. She could work and she could walk past the site undisturbed and some of the smell would wash away with the dust.

Yes, rainy days were heaven for Celeste.

Somehow, over the months, the intrusion stopped bothering her quite so much and she got more work done. Whether the noise lessened or she simply grew accustomed to it all is hard to say.

Nevertheless, it happened.

Celeste returned to her usual routine. Up with the sun, she had her morning coffee and bagel on the balcony and then headed inside for a shower and hours at the computer.

Arlene, her editor, was very pleased with this return to normal. Her fear had been that Celeste's work would suffer a permanent lapse.

Many frantic phone calls came in from Arlene about the latest manuscript. Celeste had tried every kind of manoeuvring tactic she could think of to appease her. However, Arlene continued to suffer from slight anxiety attacks.

Once talented fingers started flying over the keyboard again, Arlene had relaxed.

One morning in mid-July, she stood in the foyer of her building with one of her neighbours, Alice. Celeste had just returned from a quick trip to the bakery for fresh rolls and, once again, the rude comments from above got under her skin. She started to complain about the construction and the low-class workers on it. She truly hoped to find some sort of sympathizer in Alice.

"If those dirty, foul-mouthed Neanderthals knew how much they impacted people's lives, they would probably send a huge grunting cheer to the heavens. I can't imagine any of them giving a damn about anyone else's life outside of how uncomfortable they can make them."

Alice, her wonderfully outrageous, bohemian upstairs neighbour, who had been the first to welcome her when she moved in, simply laughed. "Oh, they're not that bad! I actually kinda like the fact that they watch my girls jiggle when I flounce past them, it feeds my ego. Besides, I get a kick outta thinking of them trying to get around up there, with massive hard-ons. Of course, in my fantasy, they are all extremely well-endowed." She held her sides as though they'd cramped from her uproarious laughter.

"Oh, Alice. That's disgusting!"

"What is?" she sobered abruptly.

"Thinking about them sexually, well endowed or not, then talking about it," Celeste huffed. "I certainly don't want to think of any of them like that."

Alice stared intently into Celeste's dark eyes and gave her two cents worth of free advice. "Girl, you need to get laid."

Astounded at her friend's bluntness, Celeste felt her face turn crimson. "What the hell is that supposed to mean?"

"Well, when's the last time you had some hot stud buried between your thighs?"

A quick, nervous glance around the small area between the front doors and the elevator assured her no one was close enough to overhear their conversation. Celeste admitted, "It has been a while. I'm too busy to even think about it."

"What's to think about?" Alice gasped. "God, if I don't get some at least three times a week I start looking at bananas and cucumbers down at the market in a whole new light. Seriously, how long has it been?"

"Well, Mike and I split up six months ago and we hadn't done anything for at least a month before the split. So I guess that makes it seven months."

"Holy shit! How do you survive that long without it? No wonder you have all this pent-up anxiety. Seriously, your insides must be damn near ready to explode from the need for release. You definitely need to have a screaming orgasm and soon, then you'll see the world in a whole new light."

The two of them stepped into the elevator. Celeste kept her eyes on the mail in her hands as though someone had sent her the big prize from the lottery and she had to figure out which envelope held the fortune.

"It is not that bad, Alice," she mumbled.

"Well, hon, once you're ready to admit that you still have a libido, give me a call. I have all kinds of friends that would be more than willing to help you chill out."

"I have seen some of those friends of yours," Celeste laughed. She pictured the unsavoury sorts she'd seen come and go from Alice's apartment. "No thanks."

"You could always just come up sometime, when I'm home alone. I am real good at relieving stress," Alice said as the doors opened on Celeste's floor. "I guarantee you would feel a hell of a lot better after."

Celeste held the door open and turned back to Alice, "While that is a very kind offer, Alice, I've always been an outy-gal. I like the feel, taste and smell of a man, the way his sexuality is right out there for all to see. It's great to see the effect I have on him with just a glance."

Alice stepped very close to Celeste and stroked her cheek affectionately. "You'll never know what you're missing in life if you don't try new things, sweetheart."

With the briefest of kisses on her cheek, Alice slipped past Celeste and skipped down the hall. "I'm gonna take the stairs," she called as she pulled the elastic from her flaming red hair. The long unruly curls fanned out behind her.

About the Author

Kandeis Lynne grew up in the Deep South as the proverbial preacher's kid. As a child, she lived up to the expectation; as an adult, she is living up to the reputation. A self-proclaimed hedonist, Kandeis uses her writing to explore ideas and feelings that her strict upbringing denied her. Kandeis is married, has a son, and teaches science in Tennessee.

www.ingramcontent.com/pod-product-compliance
Lightning Source LLC
Chambersburg PA
CBHW070535130626
46555CB00003B/1427